This book is dedicated to children all over the world,
so they may always know…

"If you're choking back tears and your heart's full of fears…
You know very well, it's OK to tell."

SWEETWATER
PRESS

Lauren's Kingdom
Copyright©2015 by Sweetwater Press

ISBN-13: 978-1-4924-6657-4

Creative direction provided by The POD and Sachs Media Group, and Claire VanSusteren.

Thanks also to Shawn Powell

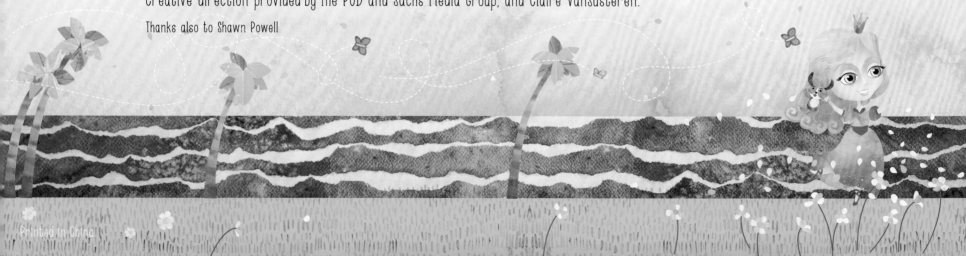

Printed in China

LAUREN'S KINGDOM

by Lauren Book

Illustrations by MARCO BARRETO

In a sunny city where palm trees sway in rhythm to the salty breeze of the mighty ocean, lived a young girl named Lauren.

Lauren's beautiful blonde hair sparkled in the sun's bright blaze, like a bouquet of dazzling yellow daffodils. Her cheery smile was so radiant that it warmed the hearts of everyone she met. Lauren was so very happy.

Lauren lived in a sweet little stone house with her family, but sometimes she would pretend her house was a giant castle that overlooked the clear blue waters of the open sea.

She would look out upon the sea and imagine she was a princess riding on the back of a friendly dolphin as the ocean's mist tickled her face.

Inside the little stone house, Lauren would pretend her bedroom was her own private palace. The walls of her room were painted pink and peach with unicorn wallpaper.

Beneath the spotlight of the bright blue moon and its twinkling sister stars, Lauren would stand on her balcony as the midnight wind would blow through her golden hair.

She would pretend this was her kingdom.

Lauren lived in the little stone house with her loving family.

Her dad was a wise and caring man who worked as a lawyer, traveling here, there and everywhere to help pass laws to make the world a better place. Sometimes, Lauren would pretend her dad was the royal king in her make-believe kingdom.

She would pretend her mom was the beautiful queen of the castle, she and her sister were princesses and her baby brother, the prince.

Lauren loved to pretend with her brother and sister. They would play hide and seek in the house, Marco Polo in the pool and a crazy game of kickball every Sunday afternoon.

At the end of the school year, Lauren's dad and mom gathered the children and announced they had hired a babysitter who would help watch the children during the summertime while school was out.

The babysitter was very nice to the children. She made them tasty dinners like chicken tenders with baby corn and angel food cake with chocolate icing for dessert.

She washed their clothes, played games with them, made them laugh and made sure they were all happy. Lauren liked the new babysitter.

One night, the babysitter entered Lauren's private palace bedroom and sat beside her on the bed. The babysitter told Lauren how beautiful her smile was. Then she touched Lauren's lips with her fingers. This made Lauren feel very uncomfortable.

The babysitter told Lauren how beautiful her hair was, and then touched Lauren's long blonde hair with her fingers.

Lauren did not feel right about the way the babysitter had touched her lips and her hair. Her tummy felt sick inside.

Every day, it seemed the babysitter was always touching Lauren where she should not be touched. Lauren could not brush her hair or even her teeth without the babysitter standing beside her.

Lauren wanted to tell someone about the way she was feeling and the way the babysitter had touched her, but she was scared of the bigger and stronger babysitter and she couldn't find the words to tell.

Lauren started staying away from her family. She did not pretend her pretty pink bedroom was a private palace...it felt more like a dark dungeon of fear and the babysitter was the terrible, green ogre holding her like a prisoner inside its walls!

Lauren's once-bright smile had faded away. No longer did she light up the faces of others when she would meet them on the street.

Lauren did not take care of her beautiful blonde hair anymore. It no longer looked like a bouquet of dazzling yellow daffodils. Sometimes she did not even wash or comb it.

Lauren even stopped eating her favorite foods like chicken tenders and angel food cake with chocolate icing.

Lauren's heart was turning to stone... she was losing her light.

One day, Lauren watched through the front window of her little stone house as her dad was climbing into the front seat of his car. She wanted to tell him what the bad babysitter was doing to her, but she felt so alone and scared.

Then she heard an inner voice - her guiding voice - speaking from her heart:

"If you're choking back tears and your heart's full of fears...
You know very well, it's OK to tell."

Suddenly, Lauren found her courage and bolted through the front door, just as her dad's car was pulling away from the curb.

She ran outside the front door to him, but she was too late. Her dad's car was already down the street.

Lauren ran down the street after him, but he did not see her.

PIER PARK

Lauren turned to make her way back home when she noticed a group of young kids playing basketball on the outside courts.

She watched as a boy her age made one basket after another. *"Good shot, Rodney!"* yelled another player.

R PARK

After the game was over, Lauren watched a man grab Rodney by the arm and hurl him to the ground.

The man yelled at Rodney, then walked away. Lauren ran to Rodney, who lay on the ground with huge tears rolling down his face.

"Are you OK?" Lauren asked.

"My uncle hates me," Rodney said sadly as he wiped his nose.

"Why don't you tell someone about the way he treats you?" asked Lauren.

"Because, he says he will hurt my mom if I ever tell her what he does to me. I have no one to help me," the young boy sniffled.

"You do now," replied Lauren.

Every day Lauren would leave her little stone house to meet with her new friend, Rodney. For the first time in months, Lauren's smile finally started to return. She began washing and combing her long blonde hair again.

Lauren would shoot hoops with Rodney. They would laugh and talk. She even found the courage to tell Rodney about her deepest, darkest secret: the mean, green ogre babysitter. He understood her pain.

Lauren made a promise to Rodney that she would tell her dad and mom about the babysitter touching her, if Rodney would tell his mom about his mean uncle hitting and kicking him. She told him: "

"If you're choking back tears and your heart's full of fears...
You know very well, it's OK to tell."

Rodney agreed, and the two friends shook hands to seal the deal.

As happy as it made the two new friends, Lauren's babysitter did not like the idea of Lauren and Rodney confiding in one another. Not one bit! So she locked Lauren inside her room to keep her from talking to Rodney ever again.

Big tears rolled from Lauren's eyes as she sat inside her dark dungeon. She curled up into a ball on her bed, closed her damp eyes and fell asleep.

Lauren dreamt she was on the back of the friendly dolphin, jumping waves and speeding through the blue-green waters of the vast ocean.

As they darted through the waters, a black cloud suddenly covered them from above. Lauren turned to find the green ogre babysitter following them on a giant barracuda.

She called out from the back of the dolphin as the waves crashed upon her tiny body. *"Help me!"* She pleaded. *"Save me from the green ogre!"*

From out of the sky, a unicorn with magnificent fiery wings sailed past Lauren and the racing dolphin. Upon the winged stallion sat her best friend, Rodney.

"I'm here for you, my friend!" he yelled.

Lauren's eyes beamed as Rodney reached down and scooped Lauren from the back of the dolphin, hoisting her up on the back of the magical, one-horned steed.

Lauren smiled as she held on to her brave friend as the unicorn flew through the snow white clouds.

When she awoke, Lauren was filled with hope. She knew that the time had come to be brave and share her unsafe secret.

So she rushed into her parents' bedroom. With tears in her eyes, Lauren took a deep breath and told her parents about the mean, green, ogre babysitter and all the terrible things she did.

Her father held his precious daughter in his arms. He looked into her eyes as tears raced down his face, *"The mean, green, ogre babysitter will never touch you again. I promise you, my sweet angel face."*

Later that night, the mean, green ogre babysitter was taken away from Lauren's little stone house forever.

Lauren was finally free to laugh and play!

The next day, Lauren looked out from her balcony to the basketball courts below and saw Rodney holding his mom's hand.

Rodney waved up to his friend Lauren. *"We did it, Lauren! We shared our unsafe secrets...even though we were scared, it was OK to tell!"*

With a smile that would outshine the brightest star, Lauren waved back to him. *"Yes, we did! Thank you, Rodney!"*

Lauren and Rodney learned a great lesson through their friendship: that it is always OK to tell a trusted adult or grown up buddy if you are feeling sad, afraid or icky.

Lauren's kingdom was a safe place now, full of love and kindness and driven by one golden rule...

"If you're choking back tears and your heart's full of fears...
You know very well, it's OK to tell."

THE END

SAFER, SMARTER KIDS ACTIVITY: TRUSTED TRIANGLE OF GROWN-UP BUDDIES

Use the **Trusted Triangle** below to identify three or more grown-up buddies that you can talk to about anything - whether it's a bad dream or a fight with a friend or a touch that makes you feel not quite right. Be sure your grown-up buddies are old enough to drive a car, and that you include at least one person in the trusted triangle who isn't a family member.

If something or someone makes you feel unsafe or not quite right, tell someone in your Trusted Triangle of grown-up buddies. It's important to remember to keep telling someone how you feel until you get the two H's: Heard and Helped.

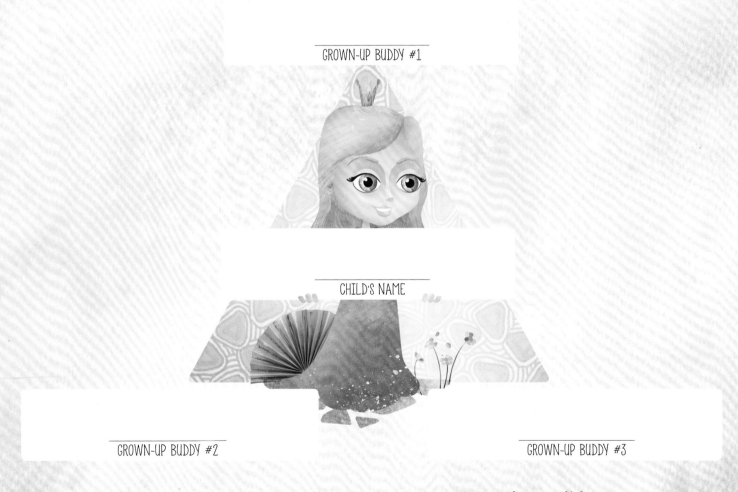

GROWN-UP BUDDY #1

CHILD'S NAME

GROWN-UP BUDDY #2

GROWN-UP BUDDY #3

For more tools and rules on how to stay safe, visit **www.LaurensKids.org**.